D1550956

Bantam Books in the Choose Your Own Adventure® Series
Ask your bookseller for the books you have missed.

#1 THE CAVE OF TIME
#2 JOURNEY UNDER THE SEA
#3 BY BALLOON TO THE SAHARA
#4 SPACE AND BEYOND
#6 YOUR CODE NAME IS JONAH
#8 DEADWOOD CITY
#13 THE ABOMINABLE SNOWMAN
#14 THE FORBIDDEN CASTLE
#18 UNDERGROUND KINGDOM
#19 SECRET OF THE PYRAMIDS
#21 HYPERSPACE
#22 SPACE PATROL
#24 LOST ON THE AMAZON
#25 PRISONER OF THE ANT PEOPLE
#26 THE PHANTOM SUBMARINE
#27 THE HORROR OF HIGH RIDGE
#28 MOUNTAIN SURVIVAL
#29 TROUBLE ON PLANET EARTH
#31 VAMPIRE EXPRESS
#32 TREASURE DIVER
#33 THE DRAGON'S DEN
#35 JOURNEY TO STONEHENGE
#36 THE SECRET TREASURE OF TIBET
#38 SABOTAGE
#39 SUPERCOMPUTER
#40 THE THRONE OF ZEUS
#41 SEARCH FOR THE MOUNTAIN GORILLAS
#43 GRAND CANYON ODYSSEY
#44 THE MYSTERY OF URA SENKE
#45 YOU ARE A SHARK
#46 THE DEADLY SHADOW
#47 OUTLAWS OF SHERWOOD FOREST
#48 SPY FOR GEORGE WASHINGTON

#49 DANGER AT ANCHOR MINE
#50 RETURN TO THE CAVE OF TIME
#51 THE MAGIC OF THE UNICORN
#52 GHOST HUNTER
#53 THE CASE OF THE SILK KING
#54 FOREST OF FEAR
#55 THE TRUMPET OF TERROR
#56 THE ENCHANTED KINGDOM
#57 THE ANTIMATTER FORMULA
#58 STATUE OF LIBERTY ADVENTURE
#59 TERROR ISLAND
#60 VANISHED!
#61 BEYOND ESCAPE!
#62 SUGARCANE ISLAND
#63 MYSTERY OF THE SECRET ROOM
#64 VOLCANO!
#65 THE MARDI GRAS MYSTERY
#66 SECRET OF THE NINJA
#67 SEASIDE MYSTERY
#68 SECRET OF THE SUN GOD
#69 ROCK AND ROLL MYSTERY
#70 INVADERS OF THE PLANET EARTH
#71 SPACE VAMPIRE
#72 THE BRILLIANT DR. WOGAN
#73 BEYOND THE GREAT WALL
#74 LONGHORN TERRITORY
#75 PLANET OF THE DRAGONS
#76 THE MONA LISA IS MISSING
#77 THE FIRST OLYMPICS
#78 RETURN TO ATLANTIS
#79 MYSTERY OF THE SACRED STONES
#80 THE PERFECT PLANET

#1 JOURNEY TO THE YEAR 3000 (A Choose Your Own Super Adventure)
#2 DANGER ZONES (A Choose Your Own Adventure Super Adventure)

THE PERFECT PLANET

BY EDWARD PACKARD

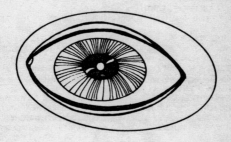

ILLUSTRATED BY LESLIE MORRILL

BANTAM BOOKS
TORONTO • NEW YORK • LONDON • SYDNEY • AUCKLAND

RL 5, IL age 10 and up

THE PERFECT PLANET
A Bantam Book / June 1988

ISBN 0-553-27227-6

Published simultaneously in the United States and Canada

Bantam Books are published by Bantam Books, a division of Bantam
Doubleday Dell Publishing Group, Inc. Its trademark, consisting of the
words "Bantam Books" and the portrayal of a rooster, is Registered in
U.S. Patent and Trademark Office and in other countries. Marca Regis-
trada. Bantam Books, 666 Fifth Avenue, New York, New York 10103.

PRINTED IN THE UNITED STATES OF AMERICA

O   0 9 8 7 6 5 4 3

THE PERFECT PLANET

WARNING!!!

Do not read this book straight through from beginning to end! These pages contain many different adventures you may have when you investigate a report of habitat unrest on the "perfect planet."

As you read along you will be able to make choices, and the adventures you have will be the results of those choices. But be careful!

Think carefully before you make a choice! A tyrant from another galaxy is out to destroy the perfect planet, and he will try to destroy you if you get in his way!

Good luck!

HISTORICAL NOTE

This book could not have been written had it not been for the courageous pioneering work of Spencer Compton, who discovered Utopa, the perfect planet, while on a mission for the Federation. It was Compton who first observed the grave troubles that arose on Utopa, and it was his report that led Federation Command to send you to investigate. That story—your story—is described in the pages that follow. As for Spencer Compton, he has been assigned by Federation Command to the University of Colorado, where he is carrying out advanced studies of the planet Earth.

While on routine patrol in the Deneb sector, you receive a transmission on the red monitor from Federation Command:

Abort patrol immediately and proceed to Utopa, fifth planet of Achnar. The planet is experiencing habitat unrest. Use extreme caution. Mike Tanner, the only other scout in your area, will join you as soon as he can get there.

Oh, no, you think, another social-adjustment mission. You hate being assigned to missions that involve interfering with a planet's natural development. But no one has asked for your opinion. As a solo scout for the Federation of Planets, your only job is to report and remedy what's wrong with troubled planets in neighboring star systems.

Your new orders are troubling for another reason. Utopa is the last place you'd expected to find unrest. By all accounts it's a paradise, notable for its peaceful inhabitants, wonderful climate, fertile land, and beautiful rivers, lakes, and mountains. In fact, throughout the galaxy, it's known as "the perfect planet."

Turn to page 39.

"Let's take it out," you say.

"Roger." Mike applies gentle thrust to the Scout, maneuvers a shade to starboard, and fires the laser cannon.

You watch in horror and fascination as the evil eye is transformed into intense blue-white light. The light is so bright that it leaves an afterimage in your brain. As it fades, you realize that the evil eye is gone, utterly vaporized. A second later you hear a sharp thunderclap.

"We got it," Mike cries. "What a weapon, just like zapping a mosquito!"

Mosquito is the last word you ever hear. Less than a second later, the Scout ship, Mike, and you are transformed into intense blue-white light.

The End

Those tree snarps may look sad and cute, but that didn't help the salika, you think as you take off through the brush. You dodge trees and stumps and soon come upon another trail. You follow it uphill, hoping you'll reach a hilltop from which you can see more of the surrounding countryside. You've got to find some Utopans soon.

Your plan of seeking high ground pays off. Soon you reach the east wall of a broad canyon. A river meanders along the grassy canyon floor. The side of the canyon opposite you is a terraced hillside, a lot less steep than the side you're on. Most of the hillside is covered with slaif plants. But you also glimpse a few round huts.

You peer over the edge of the cliff, looking for a way to get down to the canyon floor. A couple of hundred feet to your right is a rope ladder. It must have been made by the Utopans living in the little village across the canyon. When you reach the ladder, you see that it's tied around the trunk of a large tree, and it goes all the way to the bottom of the cliff. But the ropes look frayed. The ladder obviously hasn't been used in a long time.

By now you're desperately hungry. If you walk along the cliff looking for a place to get down, you might never find one. You want to get to that village. But do you dare take a chance on that old ladder?

---

*If you try to climb down the rope ladder,
turn to page 42.*

*If you search along the edge of the cliff for
another route, turn to page 101.*

A second later your computer provides the information you're looking for.

Slaif is a sturdy, thick plant with a long dark red root. It is cultivated by the Utopans with help from the mumpa beasts, gentle, heavy-set animals almost as large as elephants. Mumpa beasts have powerful forelimbs which they use to dig up the giant slaif roots. Utopans' special fingernails, stronger than steel, enable them to pare the toxic slaif skins, which taste so bitter that no animal will bite into them. Once the skins are pared, however, the pulp of the slaif is so delicious that neither the Utopans nor the animals ever tire of eating it. It is also totally nutritious, and grows so abundantly that no creature on Utopa need ever go hungry. The Utopans provide pared slaif to all creatures on the planet. Utopa is the only planet that has never experienced hunger, disaster, suffering, or war. It is the only known perfect planet.

Suddenly the screen goes blank.

Turn to page 8.

6

It seems safe on the beach now, so you wade out of the ocean. You continue on foot in the same direction, watching for mumpa beasts. You hate to leave Mike, but it would be too dangerous to go back. And there's no way you can help him now.

The shoreline curves. When you round the bend, you see the slaif forests you expected to find. To the left is a line of low cliffs pockmarked with holes big enough to walk through. They must be caves!

You know you've guessed right when you see well-worn paths leading up to several of the openings. As you get nearer, you see slaif roots scattered about, waiting to be pared.

You hurry to the nearest cave and peer inside. What you see almost stops your heart—a group of small humanoids huddled around in a circle. At last you've found the Utopans!

Turn to page 16.

As you climb the path leading up into the hills, you pass a few partially harvested slaif groves. They appear to have been abandoned.

You examine some roots lying near the side of the road. Try as you will, you can't manage to peel off the bitter-tasting, toxic skin, even with your utility knife. Now you know how frustrated the animals must feel. Slaif, slaif, everywhere, and not a bite to eat! What's happened to the Utopans? you ask yourself again and again as you trudge along the trail.

From time to time you see an animal peering at you from the forest. Within less than a mile's travel, you count six different species. You pass several animals that are as pretty and graceful as deer. But every one of them looks thin and hungry. Some of them follow you a way, as if hoping you'll pare slaif for them. You hope you don't meet any animals as angry as the mumpa beasts who attacked your spaceship.

Turn to page 11.

"State latest information," you demand.
The screen lights up again.

Recently it has been reported that Utopans have abandoned their normal work of paring slaif. This has caused starvation and never-before-seen hostility on the part of the other animals of Utopa.

You've hardly finished reading this data when a yellow light signals that your A-3 Scout ship is entering Utopa's atmosphere. You quickly adjust the restraints that will cushion you when the ship brakes.

The gentle sun is almost directly overhead as your ship lands in a meadow in a midlatitude part of the landmass. You open the hatch, hop down onto the grass, and set out immediately to look for Utopans.

Turn to page 44.

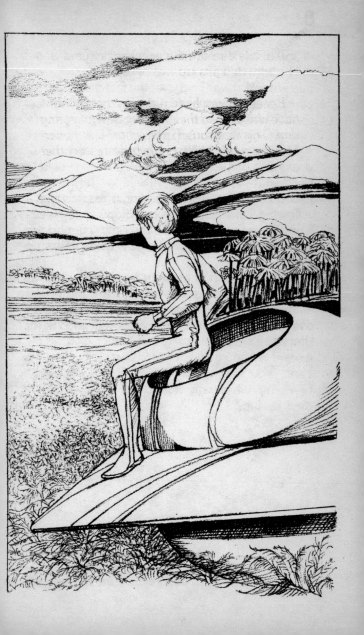

You comb through the wreckage of your Scout ship. Little is left of what was once a stunning space machine. You can't get over the fact that peaceful, gentle animals would senselessly charge a spacecraft. There's no doubt about it: Something is very, very wrong on the perfect planet.

Though your ship has been destroyed, luckily your radio transmitter is still intact. Within the hour you establish contact with Mike Tanner, the Federation scout who was sent to assist you.

During your descent your computer telemetry had advised you that you were setting down near the Green River. You relay this information to Mike.

"I'll try to land near the mouth of . . ." Mike's voice fades out as his ship enters the troposphere.

You circle the wreckage of your craft and climb to the top of a low hill. A few hundred yards away, you see a beautiful green-tinted river. You set out toward it and soon find a trail running along the bank. You feel certain you've found the Green River, but which way should you go to get to the river mouth?

If you go upstream, turn to page 13.

If you go downstream, turn to page 28.

You continue up what has now become a mountain path. You doubt if you'll find a Utopan settlement so high up. But you should reach a place where you can get a view of the countryside for miles around.

Even though you're climbing a mountain, the temperature is comfortable. Utopa still has a perfect climate. The gentle sun, always overhead, keeps you warm, and a pleasant breeze keeps you from getting too hot. You rest from time to time in the soft grass by the side of the trail. You're rapidly growing weak from lack of food and water.

If you continue on up the hill to get a look at the countryside, turn to page 15.

If you decide to turn back in search of food, turn to page 37.

12

You follow the trail for many hours. As you trudge on, you begin to wonder if you'll even survive on this planet, much less save it from utter desolation. When you hear what sounds like voices up ahead, you think you're imagining them. But suddenly the trail breaks into a clearing, and you find a group of tiny round houses with conical roofs. Several small Utopans are working together in the center square—paring slaif. A dozen or so animals—including a three-horned zetkgee and six ground snarps—are nibbling on slaif that has been set aside for them.

The leader of the village comes out to greet you. Speaking the galactic language perfectly, he tells you that his name is Ute and that you've stumbled into a remote village—the only one where people are still paring slaif. "As far as I know, the rest of the planet is starving," Ute says. "They are afraid of alien spacecraft—the eye ships—that circle overhead. But I refuse to be afraid. And my people and the animals that depend on us have been saved."

Turn to page 20.

As you walk upstream the river becomes gradually narrower. And the trail becomes rough and rocky. Ahead, you hear a faint sound. You're curious to see what's causing it. As you push your way through the thick shrubbery alongside the river, the sound grows louder. Suddenly you see white water, foaming and churning. These are rapids that no boat could navigate. It doesn't seem likely Mike would have set down in this rugged country. On the other hand, you've come this far—you'd hate to turn back now.

If you continue to follow the trail upstream, beyond the rapids, turn to page 107.

If you decide you're on the wrong track and had better head back downstream, turn to page 46.

As you continue to climb, you're amazed to find the vegetation growing ever more dense. Trees tower above you. Their huge umbrella-shaped leaves form a high canopy that allows little light to shine through. Up ahead, along the darkened trail, you hear screeching noises.

Reaching a clearing, you see a troop of small primates attacking a goatlike animal with a single long, pointed horn. You remember from your computer scan that this unicornlike creature is called a salika, and the small primates are called tree snarps. Like all the animals you've seen on Utopa, they're skinny and sickly looking. The salika gamely waves its horn, but the tree snarps are much quicker—the salika has no chance.

As you watch, the salika falls to the ground. It surely is doomed. As are the tree snarps, who don't know what to do with the carcass once they have it.

Looking at these starving, confused animals, you realize that you must help this planet help itself immediately. If you don't—or can't—all the animals will die.

You have to find the Utopans! But you feel sorry for the tree snarps. Perhaps you should try to comfort them before you leave.

If you approach the group of mourning tree snarps, turn to page 49.

If you decide to play it safe and avoid the tree snarps, turn to page 4.

16

The Utopans' large oval eyes are filled with sadness when they turn to look at you. But they seem too listless and weak to take any interest in the stranger suddenly in their midst.

Knowing that Utopans speak the standard galactic language, you call out to them. "Friends, I've been sent by Federation Command to help you—I can see your people and animals are in terrible distress. What can I do to help?"

The Utopans shrug and shake their heads. But then one—a woman holding a young child— speaks out. "We cannot go out. The eye warns us—the evil eye in the sky. We shall be cursed forever if it looks upon us."

Turn to page 110.

You can't remember the rest of Dr. Vivaldi's lecture, but you don't need to. Your computer has complete information on all planets.

You set your craft on course for Utopa, and punch an access code into your computer. The information rolls by on the monitor:

Utopa, Planet 5 of the star Achnar; Gallatin quadrant. Because it is only two-thirds the size of Earth, Utopa has delightfully low gravity. It has a large, crescent-shaped continent that always faces the planet's sun, which is less bright than Earth's sun. The result is that the planet's sunny side has constant pleasant temperatures and soft, warm light. There is a large land mass on the planet's dark side, which is presumed to be uninhabited. The ocean water on Utopa is as fresh and pure as a mountain spring. The only animals are mammals. They come in many sizes and shapes, but neither they nor the Utopan humanoids ever prey on each other. On Utopa all creatures eat slaif, and only slaif.

As your standard-issue A-3 Scout cruiser enters the orbit of the beautiful blue-green planet, you summon up more data on your computer. You're especially interested in learning more about slaif, the Utopan food.

Turn to page 5.

You dash up the beach and dive into the tall, silky grass. Rolling over and over, you try to get as far from the mumpa beasts as you can. But the crazed animals have sharp eyes. One of them veers toward you. In a moment its powerful tusks, never used before except for digging slaif roots, dig into you.

The End

"The Utopans haven't learned to fly yet," Mike says. "This thing must have come from outer space. And I'll bet it has something to do with what's wrong with this planet. But *what is it*?"

"I think I know," you say thoughtfully. "It's a manifestation of an ancient curse. The evil eye has appeared on many planets, including Earth. Each time it assumes a different form. But in every case there's an eye so evil that to look at it is to be cursed. Much has been written about this in Dr. Vivaldi's book *The History of Darkness on Earth*."

Mike seems almost frozen in awe and terror. You wonder if you'll have to take control of the Scout. But he gets hold of himself, applying braking thrusters to avoid overrunning the mysterious eye-ship.

"It's frightening," he says.

"Exactly," you say. "It's intended to frighten the Utopans. This explains why they're hiding instead of peeling slaif plants for themselves and the animals."

Mike nods. "Now we're making progress." He applies a little power to keep the Scout above stall speed of 237 mph. "Should we shoot down the evil eye?"

If you say yes, turn to page 3.

If you say no, turn to page 40.

You congratulate Ute for his courage and gratefully accept a large, freshly pared slaif root. As you munch on the delicious fruit, you feel energy flowing back into your body. While you eat, Ute talks to you as if you were an old friend.

"My followers and I settled in this remote area because we could not agree with the superstitious beliefs of the others. We felt we must fight the plague that threatens to destroy our planet." Ute bows his head, and his mouth turns down. "Glad as I am to survive this plague, I am saddened to think that all life outside our little village may be wiped out. It would be terrible to find ourselves alone on this beautiful planet—a few dozen people and perhaps a hundred animals."

Someone shouts. Ute points upward. Passing silently a few hundred feet overhead is a weird object that, more than anything else, looks like a *flying eye!*

"The curse of the evil eye," Ute says gravely. "That is the source of this plague."

Turn to page 25.

But then, in a flash of images, you see Kodor ducking to the ground, Mike groping with his fingers, the guards firing, and *Mike disappearing in a cloud of vapor*! A second later one of the guards seizes you. In a flash you realize what went wrong: Mike forgot—and you did too—that Kodor is not human, but a hominoid alien. Unlike humans, hominoids have no carotid nerve!

Before you begin to imagine what will happen to you, Kodor instructs the guards: "Dispose of the other Earthling. Now!"

The End

The Utopans begin to come out of hiding. The bolder ones set to work at a furious pace, preparing slaif, for by now thousands of animals are desperately in need of food. Admiral Gordon gives the order for the Federation task force to return to Earth; you will go with them.

"Utopa has once more become the perfect planet," Admiral Gordon says, once the *Rama* is locked on course for Earth. "At first, Kodor seemed to be a conqueror and a tyrant. Now it appears he only wanted slaif plants—just enough so he could begin to cultivate them on his own planet. He was a thief, but the planet's food supply was not impaired. Kodor may have been no more than a sophisticated drone, one of millions perhaps—space bees, buzzing around, gathering honey."

Turn to page 95.

With a last glance at the escape capsule, you strap on Mike's emergency backpack and set out along the edge of the river. You hope your emergency rations last until you can do something to help this beleaguered planet—and yourself.

You've traveled about an hour when you come upon a well-beaten trail leading uphill. Perhaps it will lead to a Utopan village.

Turn to page 12.

"What is this curse?" you ask.

Ute sighs heavily. "There is a legend that a race of enormous birds once lived on this planet. They would appear from nowhere and swoop down on their prey. These birds were clumsy and easy to dodge. But anyone who looked at one of them had no chance at all, for each bird had only one great eye. And it was an eye so filled with evil that any creature who looked at it was paralyzed with fear and became easy prey. One day, after killing many people and animals, the birds left. But according to legend, they would some day return. And now . . ." Ute looks at you helplessly.

You rest a hand on the Utopan's small, rounded shoulder. "Surely there is something we can do."

Ute looks thoughtfully at you. "If you wish, you can stay here with us. Our job will be simply to survive. Otherwise, we'll give you as much pared slaif as you can carry, and you can set out and see what you can do elsewhere."

If you stay in Ute's village, turn to page 102.

If you decide to set out again in hopes that you can convince other Utopans not to be afraid of the evil eye, turn to page 86.

Until this moment, you'd forgotten about Utopa's dark side. Since the island continent you landed on always faces the gentle and beautiful Utopan sun, the other side of the planet is dark and surely must be very cold. That's why so little is known about it, you guess. In such a climate, there could be no life, except bacteria, just as there is no life at the South Pole on Earth or at the tops of Earth's highest mountains.

You strain to remember what else you've heard about the dark side, and . . . now it comes back to you. Utopa has a moon which shines *only* on the dark side. And the moon is always full, so that even the dark side is not completely dark. Little good that will do, you think, for Utopa's moon, like Earth's, gives no heat.

Go on to the next page.

The sky grows darker as you approach the other hemisphere. Your capsule crosses the terminator, and the Utopan sun sets behind you. Ahead of you, the huge Utopan moon, tinted the most delicate shade of pink, rises above the horizon. By its rosy-hued light you see land beneath you: another continent. This one is devoid of green plants and trees but is seemingly alive with corallike growths. You can see large, fan-shaped plants gently waving. Other treelike forms seem to be made of multicolored rocks and crystals built one upon the other. In some places the land is covered with brightly tinted stones. Scattered throughout this strange landscape are a myriad of lakes, some crystalline blue, others a ghostly white—perhaps caused by mists hanging over the water.

Your sensors show that the temperature is still comfortable, even though the sun never shines on this side of the planet. The mists must be caused by the contact of cool air with warm water. The surface must be heated from within!

Turn to page 52.

As you follow the river downstream, you're struck again by the beauty of Utopa. Every tree has feathery leaves, some blue-green, some almost gold. They impart a soft, warm quality to the landscape.

Along the river are stretches of tall marsh grass. A group of deerlike animals is standing near the edge of the woods. They're bone-thin. They look at you with large, imploring eyes. You hurry on, more eager than ever to find out why things have gone so wrong on the perfect planet.

Rounding the next bend in the river, you see a broad, almost flat, stretch of hard-packed sand. Beyond it is the sea. As you watch, a golden disk-like shape—a Scout ship—skims over the water and sets down on the broad, flat beach. It must be Mike Tanner! you think. You break into a run, eager to meet your old friend.

Turn to page 64.

"The evil eye has gone!" you shout. "It will not return."

"How do you know?" someone asks.

"Federation ships have destroyed it," you reply, thinking fast.

First one, then another, then all of the Utopans step forth into the soft light of the Utopan sun. They look apprehensively about the sky. Then they kneel by the slaif roots, neatly paring away the toxic skins with their extraordinary fingernails. From time to time they pause to feed on the succulent fruit. One Utopan beckons to you. You walk over, and he hands you some slaif. You bite into it. It's indescribably delicious, and after a few more bites, you feel greatly nourished and quite satisfied.

Attracted by the scent of the harvested slaif, dozens of animals move in, eager to feed. Among them are two big mumpa beasts. They look like the same ones that killed Mike. Now they stand docilely, as they were always accustomed to doing, while they wait for the Utopans to finish preparing their slaif. Then the Utopans withdraw, and the animals move in hungrily. You smile as you watch how peacefully and happily they eat.

Turn to page 55.

"Let's get out of here," you say.

Mike ignites thrusters, setting the Scout into a deep dive.

His face is red from the g-forces pressing on his body. He speaks through tightly clenched teeth. "We're more maneuverable at low altitudes. We'll slip into a river valley and hide under the canopy of foliage."

A laser blast jolts the Scout. The ship shivers, trembles, and goes into a spin you know it was never designed to perform.

You have time to get off one last message to Federation Command: *"Beware of the Perfect Planet."*

The End

You set out, following the shoreline, walking on the grassy beach that rims the sea. Gentle waves, breaking on the tufted grass, make a pleasant musical sound.

"There's no slaif along here," Mike says. "I don't think we're likely to run into any Utopans."

"But look." You point to some impressions in the soft, moist grass. "Those are the tracks of a large animal."

Mike leans over, flicking the grass from side to side with his hand. "You're right. And they're pointed in the same direction we are. Probably made by mumpa beasts."

"Let's continue on," you say. "The mumpa beasts must have been looking for slaif, and Utopans to peel it for them."

You and Mike hurry on, eager to see where the tracks lead. You fail to notice the two huge half-starved animals charging at you.

"Watch it!" Mike screams.

You have only a split second to think.

If you run toward some nearby tall grass, turn to page 18.

If you run into the ocean, turn to page 51.

You drape yourself over the log to keep it from twisting. It's so big and heavy that soon you're able to get completely out of the water. You feel safer now. You work the log closer to the middle of the river. As you do, you find the current is running so swiftly that the log—and you with it—is being carried rapidly downstream!

You look toward one shore and then the other, trying to gauge whether you could swim to either side. You're afraid to try. Then you realize you no longer have a choice. The roaring sound up ahead can mean only one thing—rapids! You remember having seen them from the rim of the canyon before you climbed down the ladder. You hadn't realized you'd drifted so fast, and so far.

White water ahead! Waves leaping over the barely submerged rocks. You could never swim through that stuff!

Turn to page 62.

You sightly extend the little finger of your right hand, an almost imperceptible gesture that tells Mike you agree to his plan and that you'll begin the procedure within three seconds.

"Can you tell us, sir—" Mike begins.

Suddenly you're clutching at your throat, vibrating as if your body had been hit by an electric current. At the same time you fall to your right, away from Mike. All eyes are on you as you perform your act perfectly. Though you're looking away from him, you know Mike is pouncing on Kodor. You turn to look only when you hear the tyrant's scream.

Turn to page 22.

You decide that you'd better get moving. Other mumpa beasts may be attracted to the scene. You head for a grove of slaif plants, where the broad greenish-brown leaves reach to your shoulders. The slaif root itself—at least the small portion of it that protrudes above ground—is beet red.

You move forward slowly under cover of the slaif plants until you reach a forest. Here the vegetation is wilder, with strangely shaped leaves. Some of the bushes are as small as Earth radishes. Others are as large as the one-hundred-fifty-foot palm trees found on the planet Zorn. The forest trees provide excellent cover, yet they're spaced widely enough apart so that you can travel freely.

Since Mike Tanner probably won't arrive for several days, you head through the forest in search of Utopans. You soon come to a broad, heavily traveled path. It appears to be used by animals. Inspecting it closely, you see traces of wheel ruts. The Utopans are technologically primitive, but they do have carts. Undoubtedly they use this path to haul slaif.

To the left, the path appears to go up into the hills. To the right, it goes downhill. It may lead to a river, or the sea. The question is, where are you more likely to find the Utopans?

If you go left, turn to page 7.

If you go right, turn to page 12.

You've traveled only a short distance back down the trail when you hear a grunt directly behind you. It's a louder and deeper sound than you've heard from any of the animals you've encountered. You run toward a large slaif plant but before you reach it, a quadruped springs from behind a fern and into your path. The creature is only as large as a pig, but mounted on its head is a gleaming, pointed horn. Immediately another of the creatures bounds out of the woods. You pick up a heavy stick lying nearby. You back away to one side. They trot toward you, their heads down, horns aimed at your midsection.

Still another animal appears. You know you can't fight all three. You run into the woods, through groves of ferns, then leap across a creek and dive into a patch of slaif plants. You hear the animals nearby, lumbering through the ferns. An hour passes before you feel sure they've gone. Fortunately they can't pick up your scent: Animals here don't know how to smell anything except slaif.

As you try to find your way back to the trail, your body aches from fatigue, and you have a sharp empty pain in your stomach. You have water; food is what you need. You've got to find someone who can prepare the only food on this planet, slaif.

Turn to page 54.

You remember the day you first learned of Utopa at the Space Academy. In one of your courses on alien life-forms, the professor, famous astrovivologist Nera Vivaldi, had asked your class to describe a planet that could be called "a perfect planet." She'd called on you to give your answer.

"Well," you'd said, "I suppose it would be a planet like Earth, except that the people there would always be peaceful and wouldn't pollute the environment."

"That's a pretty good reply," Dr. Vivaldi had said. "But what about the animals? How do you think a zebra feels when a lion is chasing it?"

"I guess the zebra doesn't think Earth is a perfect planet," you'd admitted.

Laughter had rippled through the classroom, and Dr. Vivaldi had rapped a piece of chalk on her desk. "You may laugh," she'd said with a smile, "but for the animals that are pursued and killed, I can assure you, Earth is *not* a perfect planet."

"But could there ever be a perfect planet?" you'd asked.

"Indeed, there could be . . . and *is*," Dr. Vivaldi had said. "Its name is Utopa."

Turn to page 17.

"Let's see what else we see before we start shooting," you say.

You're pressed back against your restraints as the Scout accelerates through the stratosphere, into a low-altitude orbit.

"We'll have to do instrument scanning," Mike says. "We're too high to see any detail."

"At least our radar should have no trouble finding more of those evil eyes, if there are any," you answer. "It would be good to know how many are cruising around this planet."

"Agreed—" Mike cuts himself off as your hand comes down on his shoulder.

"Look!" you shout.

A huge gray disk above you is growing larger. It's obviously a spaceship in a higher orbit—much larger than your Scout ship and on a collision course.

"Not one of ours," Mike says. "Red alert!"

He talks into the radiocom. "This is an A-3 Scout—Federation of Planets. Please identify yourself."

Go on to the next page.

There's no reply.

"Maybe they don't hear us," Mike looks at you questioningly.

"They hear us," you answer. "They're changing orbit in a very controlled way. I suspect they have higher technology than we have."

"Then I guess we'd better not try to shoot it out with them," Mike says.

"They could have taken us out by now it they'd wanted to," you add.

Mike checks his instruments and shields. "Shall we let them approach or try to evade?"

If you say, "Let them approach,"
turn to page 48.

If you choose to evade the other ship,
turn to page 31.

As you climb down the ladder it swings, and your knees bang against the wall of the cliff. The ropes lower down look more frayed than up at the top. The rungs are hardly more than sticks, but that doesn't bother you so much. If one gives way you can grip harder on the two long supporting ropes until you can step onto the next lower rung.

But now, while you're still twenty or thirty feet from the bottom, one of the long ropes breaks! You clench the remaining rope with both hands. You can't place any weight on the rungs; they're swinging wildly in the air. And you're putting twice as much weight on the rope that held. You hook a leg around the rope to take up the strain and shinny down, bit by bit. Finally your feet touch the canyon floor!

You can't see the Utopan village because the view is blocked by trees. But you don't expect to have much trouble finding it once you cross the river, *if* you can cross the river. It's much deeper and running more swiftly than appeared from the canyon rim. You wade in up to your knees and stand there, trying to work up enough courage to plunge in. At least you don't have to worry about fish or alligators, you think. There aren't any on the perfect planet.

You spot a big log floating by. If you climb on it, maybe you can paddle your way across.

If you try to swim across, turn to page 103.

If you wade out to the log and climb on, turn to page 33.

Mike starts to say something, but cuts himself short, obviously afraid of getting another electric shock. As he glances at you, the thumb and fore-finger of his left hand form a circle—a secret signal for *Procedure 87*. Mike wants the two of you to rush Kodor, using the two-person-jump procedure you've practiced hundreds of times in space-force training. The procedure is this: You pretend to have a seizure, distracting the guards. Then Mike catapults himself forward, seizes Kodor and presses the carotid nerve in his neck. As Kodor slumps forward, Mike clasps him from behind, protecting himself from being fired upon. Then Mike holds him hostage while you disarm the guards.

Even with all your training, *Procedure 87* still seems like a long shot. But it may be your only chance.

If you try Procedure 87, *turn to page 35*.

If you decide against it, turn to page 58.

44

You've gone a few hundred yards when you hear a rumbling sound. Turning, you see two great mumpa beasts. They look like bulls but stand much taller. Their coats are long and shaggy. They're so thin you can see their ribs. And their huge brown eyes are glazed. You feel pity for them until, suddenly, they charge your Scout ship at full speed!

The impact is frightening. Two fuel lines rupture at once. Yellow flames curl out of the port thruster. A moment later the mumpa beasts and your Scout ship go up in a tremendous explosion!

You stand there for a long time, shocked by the devastation, trying to figure out what to do.

If you decide to inspect the wreckage of your craft, turn to page 10.

If you decide to continue in your search for Utopans, turn to page 36.

As you head down the trail, the river broadens and the forest gives way to a broad, grassy plain. A good landing site, you think. And sure enough, there it is: Mike Tanner's Scout ship—only half a mile ahead! You run toward it but stop short when you reach the ship. Its fins are bent, and the thruster mounts have been knocked out of line. Your heart sinks. This ship will never fly again.

Where's Mike? you wonder. Oh, no! His body is lying in the grass only a few hundred feet from his Scout. The mumpa beasts must have gotten him while he was exploring near his ship. What a disaster!

Shaking off grief and loneliness, you pay your last respects to your friend and then walk over to his ship. Inside you're relieved to find everything in good condition, including forty-two vitro bars, each designed to provide you with the nourishment you need for a day.

Go on to the next page.

As you're nibbling on a vitro bar, you thumb through the final entries in Mike's log. One entry particularly catches your eye.

0840 hours. Federation Command reports that a large, alien star-cruiser is in high orbit around Utopa. Its commander, known only as Kodor, is using robot-controlled eye ships to terrorize the Utopans so they won't come out of their caves. Kodor's ship has an advanced cloaking device and appears to have been built by aliens more technologically advanced than Earthlings. Federation ships are on their way to Utopa, but they have many parsecs to travel.

You're grateful that the fleet is on the way. But you're worried that Earth technology may not be sufficient to defeat Kodor.

Turn to page 72.

As the great disk ship approaches, you notice it's surrounded by a shell of pale green light—an anti-photon shield. The Scout's laser cannon would have been useless against it.

Mike tries again to communicate with the alien ship. Still no response. There's nothing to do now but await your fate.

The wait is not long. An oval-shaped panel on the alien ship slides open. At the same time you feel a mild, lateral acceleration—the Scout is being drawn into the huge alien ship. Your controls go black.

"They've shut off our power," Mike says.

"Ion neutralization," you reply.

The two of you exchange looks. You studied remote neutralization in space-force training. It's been worked out mathematically but never built by Earthlings. It's clear that you've been captured by aliens with technology far more advanced than your own. Your hopes of saving the perfect planet look bleak.

There's no chance for resistance. The moment the Scout enters the alien ship, your hatches are sprung, and an anesthetic gas renders you unconscious. You awaken hours later in a padded cell. Aliens, humanlike except for their cold, lifeless expressions and their rather catlike bodies, escort you to another chamber. There you're ordered to sit in chairs before a creature who, by his penetrating eyes and his air of authority, you know must be the alien leader.

Turn to page 98.

You approach the mourning tree snarps, hoping to comfort them. They look at you curiously. You stand very still. Very cautiously the small animals move toward you with tearful eyes. One of them hops up onto your shoulder and makes itself comfortable at the crook of your neck. It's so cute and furry, you let it stay. Another one follows. Soon all the snarps are clinging to your statuelike body. Once again they sing their low, mournful song.

The moaning and singing continues—for longer than your patience can bear. You decide to take the furry little things off you, one by one. You've hardly begun when the snarps dig their sharp little teeth into your flesh. There are so many of them you have no time to protect yourself. It's a quick execution—you don't ever have time to scream.

Afterward the furry little snarps mourn your death.

The End

You run toward the ocean—not thinking about whether it will be cold or warm, or even safe to swim in. You wade in up to your knees, plunge, and swim as hard as you can. Only when you're almost out of breath do you stop and look back. The mumpa beast that chased you is standing on the shore. Apparently, it doesn't like the water, and that fact has saved your life. But Mike wasn't so lucky. He lies dead, gored by the other animal, which now stands over him, not knowing what to do after its senseless act.

You swim parallel to the shore, hoping the mumpa beast won't follow. The water is warm and fresh and clean. If it weren't for what happened to Mike, you'd really enjoy swimming on Utopa. When you next look around, the mumpa beasts are moving off in the other direction. They're walking slowly, with their heads low, as if they understood that their violence was wrong and useless.

Turn to page 6.

A few hundred kilometers farther on, your capsule, its fuel almost exhausted, sets gently down on the sparkling, corallike surface. To your surprise you are quickly surrounded by small, green-skinned humanoids who look much like the Utopans on the other side of the planet. They eagerly greet you, all talking at once.

You learn that these creatures live both in the water and on the land. They sleep in special chambers underground, where they're kept warm by heat flowing up from deep within the planet. And they get all the food they need from the minerals found in abundance around all the lakes. These friendly creatures feed you and promise to take good care of you until help comes.

"Your world is the most beautiful I've ever seen," you tell Ondine, their leader.

"Yes," she says, smiling. "It is true—Utopa is the perfect planet."

You smile to yourself. Ondine has no idea that Utopans live on the other side of the planet. Yet you were just as narrow in your own thinking. It never occurred to you, after all, that intelligent people might be living on the dark side of Utopa. And unless Federation Command thinks of that possibility, you'll never be rescued.

The End

"Listen. You must listen to me," you plead. "I feel sure the evil eye was placed in the sky to frighten you. As one of our great Earth leaders once said, 'You have nothing to fear but fear itself.' If you come out and prepare the slaif, you and the animals will have a chance of surviving. But if you just hide in your caves, you will surely die."

To your dismay, none of the Utopans move. They seem paralyzed by fear. Again and again you plead with them. Still, no one makes a move.

Your eyes meet those of the woman cradling the young child in her arms. Her eyes are blurred by tears, and your heart goes out to her. You hold out a hand.

"I will try it," she says. "I cannot bear to see my child starve while I do nothing."

The woman walks out of the cave and lays her child gently on the grass. Then, while you watch in amazement, she bends over a slaif root. Her steel-hard nails extend like a cat's claws as she brings her fingers down, raking them along the smooth brown tuber, and the toxic skin peels off. Eagerly she bites into the succulent root. She claws out some pulp and places it in her baby's outstretched hand.

Turn to page 65.

At last you find the trail and continue on your way. As the hours pass, your body grows numb, your vision starts to blur, and your ears can only detect the desperate poundings of your heart. You're out of the forest now, and the trail continues on through beautiful meadows. But your strength is waning.

Finally your legs buckle and your body falls on the soft warm soil of Utopa. As you lie peacefully on your side, your muscles relax. Nearby is what looks like a large, furry rock. You strain to focus your eyes. When you do, you realize the "rock" is a wality, a huge gopherlike animal, stricken with the same fate as you. Neither you nor the wality can go any farther. Looking up at the beautiful blue sky of Utopa, you join it in peaceful death.

The End

Suddenly the air is pierced by a scream. You look first at the Utopans, then up at the sky—and see an ovoid-shaped object on which is painted a huge distorted eye. The evil eye! The screaming Utopans are already running toward their cave.

Panicked by the uproar, the animals stampede. And you're directly in the path of a mumpa beast!

The End

56

You and Mike prepare to take off in his Scout ship, with you in the copilot's seat. Normally the copilot would be a Starthinker computer, but Mike has placed the Starthinker on standby.

"We're in a novel situation," he says. "Human thought and judgment are needed more than high-speed electronics now."

Glancing out the view port you see a herd of mumpa beasts. And they're charging!

"Let's get out of here." You nudge Mike's arm.

In a second the thrusters ignite. A moment later the ship lifts off.

Since the Scout can't operate efficiently at sub-orbital altitudes, your near-view of Utopa will be limited. You strain to see as much as you can of the planet's surface during the ship's rapid climb through the atmosphere.

Altitude 5,000 . . . 10,000 . . .

"Cut off thruster!" you yell at Mike. An object has caught your eye—flying along the coast only a few hundred feet off the ground.

"See it!" Mike answers, cutting off power and letting the Scout coast. He brings the ship around in an arc to close in on the object from above and behind. "What is it?"

You stare openmouthed, unable to reply. The object is ovoid shaped, perhaps twenty meters long, and has the appearance of a human eye. But not an ordinary eye. Its proportions are distorted as if reflected in a bent mirror. It's a horrifying and disturbing sight.

Turn to page 19.

By the slightest movement of your little finger, you let Mike know that you don't want to try to jump Kodor. Instead, you speak directly to the tyrant.

"How do you plan to use us?" you ask.

Tapping his clawed fingers together, Kodor allows a thin smile to cross his face. "You have already noticed, I presume, that when I conquer a planet I try to avoid damaging it. I don't like to destroy property that will eventually be mine."

"That's what you're doing on Utopa?"

Kodor nods. "Exactly. I could vaporize the Utopans and those bothersome animals out of existence. Instead I prefer to let them starve themselves."

"That eye ship—it has something to do with it, doesn't it?" Mike speaks in such a challenging way that you're afraid Kodor will give him another electric shock.

Go on to the next page.

But the tyrant seems to enjoy gloating about how smart he is.

"Exactly, my young Earthling." he says. "Every Utopan is convinced that long ago great birds ravaged the land. Each of them had only one terrible eye. To look at it meant death. In Utopan mythology the evil eye is the greatest curse that could occur. I knew that when these primitive people saw my eye ships they would hide in their caves. They would not prepare slaif for the animals or for themselves. All life would end—without the slightest damage to my future property." Kodor punctuates his utterance with a laugh so loud it hurts your ears.

Turn to page 108.

60

At last an idea comes to mind. "It may be true, Kodor, that you have superior might," you say. "But you haven't asked your computers all the questions you should. If you had, you'd know that on Earth very bad things happen to conquerors. *On Earth, the greater the conqueror, the more terrible is his defeat!*"

"Wha . . . ? How can this be?" Kodor's alien face turns purple with anger. "You lie to me!"

Your whole body shakes as you feel a fierce jolt of electricity course through you. You don't know whether you could stand another shock like that but you can't give in now.

"Ask your computers about the greatest conquerors in Earth's history," you say, looking Kodor in the eye. "Ask about Alexander the Great, Caesar, Napoleon, Hitler!"

"Lock the Earthlings up!" Kodor commands.

In an instant, the clawed fingers of a guard dig into your shoulder. Your body goes limp as you're dragged away. There's no use struggling. Your last hope is gone.

Turn to page 75.

You begin to send out a standard interlog, a message to all points—*"Do you hear me?"*—hoping that whoever controls the eye ships will respond.

Within seconds you receive a message: *"Earthling, your message is acknowledged. This is Kodor, regent of the galaxy. We have been monitoring your every move. Our command ship, made invisible behind an ion shield, will pass over you in eighty-three Earth seconds. We shall drop our shield so you can see our ship."*

Turn to page 69.

62

You've got about a minute until you reach the rapids. Slowly, carefully, you crawl forward on the log until you reach your goal—the stub of a broken-off limb. You lie flat, wrap your arms around the stub and hold on! Suddenly the log is whirling through the rapids, rolling and pitching in every direction! Spray hits your face as if someone had turned a fire hose on you.

Thunk! You feel a shock and have to use all your strength to keep from being thrown forward as the log collides with a rock. Then the log jerks sideways, stopped for a moment as it's caught between two rocks. An ocean of water pours over you. Still you hold on. In a moment the log breaks free and careens on through the rapids. How long will this last? you wonder. You know you can't hang on forever. Another wall of water washes over you, and then . . . all is calm. You're through the rapids. And once again your log is drifting serenely downstream.

Turn to page 113.

64

Mike's landing is perfect. In a few minutes the two of you are reunited.

"I flew over a Utopan village," Mike says, "but it was deserted. They must be hiding in the forests or in caves."

"That may be why the animals are starving," you say. "The Utopans are failing to pare the slaif roots for them."

"It's our job to find out what's happening," Mike says. "It seems to me that we have two options: We can take this Scout ship up and orbit the planet, or we can explore on foot.

"Unfortunately" he adds, "we can't cruise at suborbital altitude—we'd use too much fuel."

If you say, "Let's explore Utopa from orbit,"
turn to page 56.

If you say, "Let's set out on foot,"
turn to page 32.

You smile as you watch the child devour the tasty morsels. In a few seconds the Utopan woman has prepared far more slaif than she and her baby can eat. You scoop out a chunk of slaif with your fingers and hungrily bite into it. It's delicious, and after only a few bites your hunger is satisfied.

The other Utopans had been cautiously watching from the cave. Now they rush out and attack the slaif roots, paring off the toxic skins with lightning speed. You move back a way, watching with pleasure. Then you notice a few animals standing at the edge of the brush. Undoubtedly they were attracted by the enticing aroma of freshly peeled slaif. Among the animals are two huge mumpa beasts. For a moment you're afraid they'll charge. But they stand patiently, like docile horses, apparently content that the Utopans are again preparing slaif, as they always have.

Suddenly a Utopan lets out a cry of alarm. You look up in the sky—and see an ovoid-shaped object that looks like a huge distorted eye. The eye ship! The Utopans quiver like frightened rabbits.

You jump up on a rock. "It's all right! You have nothing to fear!" you yell.

Turn to page 100.

Encouraged, and perhaps ashamed of themselves, others emerge from the cave and start paring slaif. Several thank you and offer you more of the delicious fruit than you can eat.

You've saved this village and the animals that depend on it. But you know that's not enough. You gather the villagers together and begin to talk. Finally you convince them to go outside their village and persuade Utopans everywhere that they have nothing to fear.

Turn to page 112.

"Call up the Space Fleet," you order. "I'm not going to let the only perfect planet in the universe go to wrack and ruin," you tell your staff. "We'll take out the zetkgees and restore Utopa to what it was!"

The next day dozens of Space Fleet fighters crisscross the Utopan landscape, firing shafts of deadly light at the hapless zetkgees. The remains of their bodies pile up in dreadful heaps. But despite the fantastic capabilities of your fighter craft, many zetkgees escape into dense undergrowth or into caves, and many other animals are hit by mistake. Terrified by the mayhem, the mumpa beasts stampede and cause vast damage to Utopan villages. Other animals jump over cliffs or into the ocean to escape the deadly peril. The surviving Utopans take to caves.

You watch the progress of your campaign on the video monitor. But you're sickened by what you've done. Ruefully you call off your forces and head your fleet back toward Earth, leaving Utopa in rotting ruins. There's no such thing as a perfect planet, you think as you stand looking out at the stars, and there never can be.

The End

On hearing this, you open the hatch on Mike's Scout and look upward. The bright blue sky is empty. Suddenly a sizable portion of sky is blotted out! A huge disk-shaped object is drifting overhead! Though it can't be more than a few hundred feet off the ground, it appears to be smooth and seamless. There are no wings or engines or thrusters—obviously it's a product of very advanced technology. You realize how hopeless it would be for you to try to combat this ruthless alien in Mike's Scout. Kodor's power might be too formidable even for the combined forces of the Federation.

You radio back: *"Respectfully request: What are your intentions?"*

"We will take seven hundred slaif plants back to the planet Nantor."

"Why are you terrifying the Utopans?" you ask. *"You must realize that they and all the animals on this planet will starve if you don't remove the eye ships."*

"We know that," Kodor replies. *"We never harvest plants from a planet until we kill all the troublesome creatures on it. This we do by simply letting them destroy themselves. You see, we always do things as efficiently as possible. That is why I am regent of the galaxy."*

Turn to page 109.

70

You swim as hard as you can, courageously battling the current as you try to reach the other side. Too late you realize that you're using most of your energy just to stay in the same place. You feel the strength leaving your body. You struggle harder. Then a small, rippling wave chokes your breath. Your struggle is over.

The End

"We'll separate the zetkgees from the other creatures," you tell your staff. "I'm not willing to exterminate a whole species of innocent animals."

You order up a shuttle craft. Moments later you land in the midst of the largest community of Utopans, now settled in the northwestern edge of the island-continent. You find these poor creatures confused and frightened. Many have fled from other areas that have been overrun by zetkgees. The Utopans are primitive in their ways and quite superstitious, but they're also quite intelligent. They readily understand that they're in danger of being wiped out by the rapidly multiplying zetkgees. When you outline your plan to erect a wall that will seal off the peninsula from the rest of the island continent, they quickly agree.

You issue orders for a brigade of construction robots to build the wall. Most of the Utopans and the other animals are thereby saved from being starved out by the zetkgees, who keep multiplying until they've eaten almost all the slaif on their side of the wall. From then on, the zetkgee population drops until it's balanced with the food supply.

The Utopans and other animals continue to live the way they used to on their side of the wall, while the three-horned zetkgees occupy the main part of the island continent. Utopa is once again at peace. But it can no longer be called a perfect planet: No planet can be perfect when its stability depends on a wall.

The End

You know it will take weeks for other Federation ships to reach Utopa. You and Mike were the only units in the entire Deneb sector.

As the days pass you spend a lot of time watching out the ship's view port, looking for one of Kodor's eye ships to pass over. You don't know how many are circling the planet, but you observe that one of them passes overhead every few hours. As long as they do, you know the Utopans won't come out of their caves, and the animals won't be able to eat.

That sad fact is confirmed again and again when you see one or another creature—tree snarps, web-footed queetars, three-horned zetkgees, and an occasional mumpa beast—peering out of the bushes that ring the clearing where Mike's Scout ship set down. When you first see a mumpa beast, a shiver of fear runs through you. You remember how, moments after your own Scout landed on Utopa, two crazed beasts charged it, setting off an explosion that destroyed them and your ship. But your fear turns to pity when you look at these creatures. They're so emaciated and weakened by hunger they're barely able to stand, much less do any damage.

On the forty-fourth day, your radio receiver comes to life: a standard approach interrogatory. You activate a narrow homing beam following Federation pulse-code procedures. With a little luck one of the new stealth crafts will be setting down beside you in a few days!

Turn to page 93.

You order your task force to set course for Earth without delay. It would be impossible to save the perfect planet from the law of the jungle. Anyway, you tell yourself, a planet that needs to be saved can't be called perfect to begin with. There are thousands of other problems in the galaxy more pressing than this one.

You'll try to put Utopa out of your mind and accept reality: The perfect planet is an impossibility.

Turn to page 106.

Hours have passed since you and Mike were separated. You're alone in a detention cell, thinking of all the friends you'll never see again when two guards dressed in scarlet fatigues pull you out of the cell and march you back to the control room. Once again you stand before Kodor. You wonder why he's bothering to talk to you before he executes you. Then you notice that he looks pale and tired. His purplish face looks thinner and older. The regent of the galaxy looks strangely vulnerable.

"You were right," Kodor begins, his voice quivering. "For some reason, the greatest conquerors on Earth have always *lost*. Our computer-stored history of Earth shows that the first of the great conquerors, Alexander, had no sooner vanquished the world than he was destroyed by bacteria. Julius Caesar, the next great conqueror, was stabbed to death by his closest friend. Napoleon no sooner conquered all of Europe than most of his army died of cold and starvation. Finally, Hitler, the most terrible conqueror of all, failed to break the will of the peaceful people of the world, and he shot himself in a dusty cellar."

"What your computer tells you is true," you say. "Each of these conquerors had the greatest military might in the world; yet each was himself conquered."

Turn to page 91.

"Admiral, I think we should wait awhile. We don't have enough information to make a decision," you say. "It's like rolling dice, and that's no way to play with the fate of Utopa, much less the fate of the Earth. If we're stronger than Kodor, it won't hurt us to wait. We may learn a lot, and what we learn may save us."

Admiral Gordon looks at you intently. "You speak wisely, my young friend," he says. "We won't make a move for the moment. Deploy all sensors at maximum strength," he orders the watch officer.

Turn to page 104.

As you approach the Scout ship, you see at once that it will never fly again. The main thruster is badly damaged, either because of a mishap on landing or an attack by mumpa beasts. The hatch is open, but there's no sign of Mike. And no message for you. It doesn't seem likely he would have gone far from the ship without leaving you a message. He may have run into trouble while exploring nearby, you think.

You try the radio. Useless. The aerials have been destroyed.

For a few moments you'd forgotten how hungry you were. Now you raid the Scout's larder. There's at least a five-week supply of vitro bars and supplements in the pantry. You also find Mike's backpack, filled with emergency rations. The fact that he didn't take it when he left the ship is almost sure proof that he didn't intend to go far.

Turn to page 89.

It's 0559 hours aboard the *Rama,* which will be the prime observation post for the battle—a battle that in the age of laser destroyers may last only a few millionths of a second. In less than a minute now, if all goes well, Kodor's command ship will be transformed into its constituent atoms. Of course, it's possible that Kodor possesses some terrifying system that will destroy all Earth forces. But in all things one must take risks, especially in warfare.

0559 + .

"Standby."

"FIRE."

0600. Violent, flashing streaks of light dance around Kodor's ship. You fix your eyes on the computer simulation on the video screen, not on the live image, because too much of what is happening is in the form of nonvisible electromagnetic radiation. In slow motion you watch Kodor's ship being blown to atoms!

Victory!

Turn to page 116.

"What do you want—" Mike starts to ask. Suddenly he reels backward in his seat, his mouth half open, his lips drawn tightly over his teeth. He slumps in his seat, a cold sweat on his face. You know that Kodor administered another electric shock. He didn't like Mike's question or his tone or, maybe, he just wanted to show his power.

"Your level of technology is far beyond anything we've ever seen," you comment.

A thin smile plays across Kodor's face. "Yes, my power is almost unlimited. Your Federation of Planets will soon be under my control. You two have been spared—for the moment—because I intend to use you in my plan of conquest."

You tilt back in your chair, shocked as you realize your mission now is not just to save Utopa, but to save Earth itself!

Turn to page 43.

Furious, you pick up a stick and head for the caves on the far side of the village. Just as you suspected, you find a dozen or more Utopans huddled inside a cave. They look as emaciated and pathetic as the animals they've deserted. They all speak the galactic language, but that doesn't mean you can communicate. No matter what you say, they keep muttering about the evil eye. They just won't believe that they have more to fear from their own inaction than from the eye ships.

Finally, in total frustration, you grab the arm of a Utopan boy and drag him outside the cave. The Utopans, who never fight with each other, cry and gesture. But no one makes a move to stop you as you lead the unwilling boy out to the center of the village.

"Please, let me go back," he pleads.

"Not until you've pared enough slaif for yourself and your family," you say.

The boy looks up at the sky with wild, frightened eyes. But then, without a word, he kneels beside a slaif root and with a few swift, slicing motions pares off its skin with his fantastically adapted fingernails. Though just a child—and in a weakened condition at that—it takes him only a few minutes to pare enough slaif to feed everyone in the cave.

Turn to page 66.

Many years have passed since you were a young scout on a mission to Utopa. In that time you've risen through the ranks. Now you're commodore of the Federation, with the greatest fleet in the galaxy under your command. Thanks to your brilliant leadership, the sun's area of the galaxy is at peace, and Earth people have nothing to fear from alien forces. Under these conditions, your role as commodore is not to win battles but to prevent hostilities from arising.

There are still many unexplored parts of the galaxy. And no one can be sure that some evil genius is not at work somewhere, plotting the conquest of the spiral arm that holds the sun. The Federation sends thousands of probe craft out each year, seeking intelligence in unknown realms. And your spaceships must be constantly updated, and new battle techniques learned, so that if ever a threat should arise, the Federation Space Fleet will be ready.

Go on to the next page.

A bright spring morning at the Lochmoor Space Base near Carthage, Missouri, finds you going over the latest intelligence reports from the Omega sector. One seemingly routine report brings a scowl to your face. For the first time since you were last there, trouble has been reported on Utopa, the perfect planet. The report reveals that the trouble arises not from some alien force, but from creatures on the planet itself. A mutated species—the three-horned zetkgees—have become immune to the toxic skin of the slaif root. They are, therefore, able to eat slaif without help from the Utopans. As a result, the number of zetkgees on Utopa has been growing steadily. Presently there's no great problem—there's still plenty of slaif for all the creatures on Utopa. But, since there are no predators on Utopa, there's nothing to stop the zetkgees' population growth. They threaten to overrun the planet, consuming slaif at an alarming rate.

Turn to page 115.

84

You stow about half the food supply aboard the escape capsule (you haven't the heart to take all of it since there's a very slight chance Mike might return). Then you open the escape portal, strap yourself into the capsule, and check out the controls.

Activate.

All systems functional, the computer reports.

It's now or never! you think.

Full Initial Thrust.

The capsule's main purpose is to get a space pilot out of a hopeless situation. It's designed to eject with tremendous acceleration. As the tiny vehicle blasts out of the A-3 Scout, you feel as if you're being squashed into your seat. The capsule screams across the river and climbs over the hills. You throttle back and try to set the capsule on a curving course that will enable you to survey the island continent and look for a Utopan village. But the rudder is jammed! You can't turn. And you can't land—you're over the ocean. Traveling at supersonic speed, the escape capsule heads for the dark side of the planet.

Turn to page 26.

As *Omricon* slides into a comfortable orbit around Utopa, your scanners transmit a series of computer-enhanced images of the planet's surface. The situation has deteriorated far more than you'd feared. The three-horned zetkgees are everywhere. Millions of acres of slaif forest lie stripped and bare. The Utopans and other animals have been driven to a few remote areas. Already their supplies of slaif are growing scarce. They all look well nourished. But it's obvious that they must spend more and more time each day searching for slaif where once they could find it in abundance growing close at hand. Life on the perfect planet is turning into a nightmare. You pace back and forth in the control room of the flagship wondering what you can do.

If you decide to order your attack forces to exterminate most of the zetkgees, turn to page 67.

If you try to set up a preserve and wall off the zetkgees from the Utopans and other animals, turn to page 71.

If you decide to try to turn your ship into sort of a Noah's ark and take some Utopans and other animals and a quantity of slaif plants on board and set them up on some other planet, turn to page 94.

If you feel that it's futile to try to keep Utopa as the perfect planet and decide to just let nature take its course, turn to page 73.

86

As you prepare to set out on your journey, Ute tells you that after a few hours walk you will come to another village.

"Perhaps you can persuade those villagers not to be afraid of the eye ships," he says. "But I doubt it. More likely you will find them hiding in the nearby caves."

You're feeling so good after having a few hearty meals of slaif that you're quite optimistic as you hike through the beautiful forest. But when at last you reach the Utopan village, you're stunned by the sight before you. The village is deserted. All the huts and cabins have been demolished. Probably, you guess, by a herd of stampeding mumpa beasts. Almost sadder still, a dozen or so three-horned zetgkees in various stages of malnutrition are pawing at chunks of slaif root, pathetically trying to pare off the toxic skin. When they see you they stop pawing at the roots and look up at you with mournful eyes.

You feel sorry for the poor creatures and angry at the Utopans for deserting them. And you're furious at whatever alien force has sent its eye ships to terrorize the innocent Utopans. You bend over and angrily jab your knife into the skin of a small slaif root. Your knife blade snaps. The zetgkees look on helplessly—they just don't understand.

Turn to page 80.

88

You say nothing for a moment. You know the time for decision has come, and the fate of Utopa hangs in the balance.

Admiral Gordon lays a hand on your shoulder. "Look, you were on the planet awhile. What would you do? I'm inclined to attack Kodor's command ship unless you can think of a good reason not to."

If you choose to advise attack, turn to page 96.

If you advise waiting, turn to page 76.

After you eat a couple of vitro bars, your energy begins to return. The outlook is bleak but there is one possibility. The Scout is equipped with an escape capsule—a rudimentary shuttle craft designed to make brief moon-to-moon hops. Or in an emergency, to keep a pilot alive in space for a few days. It wouldn't even begin to take you back to Earth. Normally it couldn't be launched from a Scout on the ground. But Mike's ship touched down with the launching bay facing the river. There's a fair chance you could launch the escape capsule so that it would clear the hills beyond the opposite shore. Then, if all went well, you could make a suborbital flight over Utopa, as far as halfway around the planet. Attempting a launch, however, could also bring a quick end to your hopes.

If you attempt to launch the escape capsule, turn to page 84.

If you decide not to risk it, turn to page 24.

For the next hour, the radio beams a continuous full-spectrum, code four distress signal toward Federation Command Center. Then the transmitting batteries run out.

The days go by, and all goes well. The Utopans are harvesting slaif, and the animals look much healthier in only a few days. Many Utopans visit you bringing gifts of trinkets and blankets and, of course, all the slaif you can eat. Occasionally an eye ship flies by, but by now the Utopans have overcome their fear and rarely look up when it passes overhead.

Then the signal you've been waiting for comes through: *"Message received. Battle fleet on the way to deal with enemy."*

You let out a yell of joy, which you cut short when a strange voice comes over the radio: *"This is Kodor, regent of the galaxy. You have sought to interfere with my supreme rule of the planet Utopa. The penalty is death."*

The transmission ends. All is silent. But you have little doubt that your own fate is sealed. You can only hope Federation forces will be strong enough to defeat this tyrant before it's too late— and there's no one left alive on the perfect planet.

The End

Kodor heaves an enormous sigh. "I just do not understand it—but I am a supremely logical creature and therefore I must accept the fact that conquering Earth is unwise."

You're more than pleased to hear this, and inspired to say more:

"If you're supremely logical, Kodor, why are you conquering Utopa?"

"No harm will come to me if I conquer Utopa," Kodor says testily. "And I need seven hundred slaif plants for my space station."

"But you don't need to kill for that," you exclaim. "There's plenty of slaif to spare on the planet. The Utopans have always lived peacefully with other creatures on their planet. They'd be glad to let you have all the slaif you need for your space station!"

Kodor looks around, obviously puzzled. "Hmm . . . If what you say is true, then it would be illogical to conquer the planet."

"Therefore, I'm sure you won't," you reply. "Because, as you said, you're supremely logical."

Kodor looks at you intently with his great, gaping eyes. "You have spoken well, Earthling." Turning to a lieutenant he says, "Remove the eye ships from the planet of Utopa. Send an ambassador to the Utopans to arrange for our getting the slaif we need for our space station."

"You've acted wisely, Kodor," you say. "Now, once again, Utopa will be the perfect planet."

The End

Three days later a robot stealth craft sets down on the grass near your ship. Your sensors only register its presence at the very last moment.

Following instructions, you board the stealth craft and proceed to the *Rama,* the Federation flagship. The *Rama,* one of the largest and most powerful ships in the fleet, is posted a few million miles away.

Admiral Herbert Gordon welcomes you aboard. A portly, balding man with twinkling blue eyes, the admiral is clearly approaching retirement age. He questions you about your experiences on the perfect planet while giving you a tour of his ship. Suddenly a young officer runs up with a message.

"Admiral, our scouts have just reported that Kodor's command ship has set down on the surface of Utopa. Several robots have begun loading slaif plants aboard. Kodor is not just taking slaif, but whole plants—dirt, roots, and all."

"That could be good news, Admiral," you observe. "If Kodor can grow his own slaif, he won't have to keep raiding Utopa."

"Maybe so," Admiral Gordon says, "but right now, Kodor's eye ships are still circling the planet, and the Utopans and all the animals are starving to death. We may have to try to destroy the aliens' command ship and Kodor with it. I know he has extremely advanced shields, but I think our weapons are superior."

Turn to page 88.

You order a large transport ship—which you nickname the *Ark*—to land in the middle of the island continent. Your robot teams set about digging up slaif plants and bringing them aboard. You've already obtained the permission of Federation Council to relocate a few Utopans onto the planet Oroa, Deneb sector, along with members of all the species of Utopa, except for the three-horned zetkgees. Some of the mumpa beasts pace back and forth and paw the ground at the sight of your approaching robots. But eventually two docile mumpas clamber aboard the *Ark*. Otherwise, loading goes smoothly. The most difficult problem you have is in deciding which Utopans to bring aboard. Finally you select a few fine representatives of these primitive humanoids. The rest must be left behind to face the rising "flood" of the three-horned zetkgees.

When the loading is completed, the *Ark* takes off and sets course for Oroa, which you hope will become the new perfect planet. Perhaps it will be that for awhile, you reflect as your ship streaks back toward Earth. But you know that someday a new problem will arise. It could come at any time: a problem like that caused by Kodor, or by the multiplying zetkgees, or some problem you can't even imagine. For in truth, the idea of a perfect planet is only a dream.

The End

About three weeks later your spaceship breaks through the Earth's atmosphere and sets down at the Lochmoor Space Base near Carthage, Missouri. As always, you're overcome by a joyous sense of wonder and appreciation on landing back on your home planet.

A few days later you meet with your old professor Dr. Nera Vivaldi. She is, of course, eager to hear about your trip to Utopa.

"It's strange," you say. "Even though Utopa is a perfect planet, and Earth is extremely imperfect, I'd much rather live on Earth than on Utopa."

"I feel the same way," Dr. Vivaldi says. "The truth is, perfection is only an illusion. Dealing with imperfection is what life is all about."

The End

"Let's attack!" you say.

The admiral frowns, then slowly nods in agreement. "I think you're right, though the prospect of attacking is frightening. We don't know what powers Kodor has."

"All the more reason for us to attack," you say. "We need the advantage of surprise."

Admiral Gordon, scowling, rubs his chin. "It's true we'll need every advantage."

The next few hours are spent in strategy sessions with the admiral's top aides. The major problem is figuring out how to penetrate Kodor's awesome ion shields.

Mark Sterber, chief science officer of the *Rama*, states the problem clearly: "Any electronic emanation sends out a series of nonpalpable waves ahead of it. Kodor's shield is so advanced it can detect these harmless waves before a single laser photon can reach its target."

"How much warning does the wave detector give them?" you ask.

Sterber consults his notes. "About a millionth of a second, but that may be all they need. The question is how to deprive them of that millionth-of-a-second warning."

Go on to the next page.

"Well," you say, "why not a perfectly coordinated attack from multiple points? Kodor's wave sensors will refer the various waves to a computer, and the reactive force will be delayed until computer analysis is completed. Analysis is critical in such a system. Otherwise, a huge defensive discharge might inadvertently occur in the event of a magnetic storm."

"Hmm, I see what you mean," Admiral Gordon says. "Kodor's analysis will take more than a millionth of a second."

You punch several factors into the computer. Thirty seconds later you read the data. "Three-point-five millionths of a second, even working at theoretical limits. Enough time for our laser beams to do their work!"

"I think you've got it!" The admiral's fist comes down on the table. "We'll attack tomorrow at oh-six-hundred hours."

Turn to page 78.

"My name is Kodor," this imperious creature begins. "Regent of the galaxy."

"And we are—"

Kodor cuts you off with a wave of clawed fingers, sending an electric shock through your body. His voice is hard as steel. "You needn't tell me who you are. I know everything."

You try to keep your fear from showing. But your hands grow clammy. You can feel your heart beating faster. Your fear is not only for your own life, but for the whole Federation of Planets. Yet you mustn't surrender to fear and panic. There is, at least, one glimmer of hope. Kodor could have killed you—could have destroyed the Scout in an instant. But he didn't. Maybe you have some bargaining power after all.

Turn to page 79.

The Utopans listen! They watch nervously as the eye ship drifts overhead and passes out of sight over the horizon. Then they resume work on the slaif roots. Soon they have all had their fill, and the animals move in to take their turn.

One of the Utopans walks up to you. "We are very grateful to you. We shall spread the word among the rest of our people." He puts out his hand.

If Utopans were capable of aggression, those fingernails could shred your wrist in a single movement, you think. You shake the clawed hand.

"The evil eye did not harm us," the Utopan says, "but why does it circle our planet like this? What does it mean?"

You shake your head. It's clear you haven't yet solved the Utopans' problems. Whoever is behind the evil eye may soon try other means to destroy these gentle people.

The following day, the Utopans help you find your way back to Mike's Scout ship. Fortunately, no mumpa beasts have attacked it while you were gone. You switch on the radio.

If you set the radio on continuous distress call to the Federation, turn to page 90.

If you decide to try to make radio contact with the power behind the evil eye, turn to page 61.

Hour after hour you walk along the rim of the cliff. You're heading toward the sea, and you would expect the terrain to become more gentle. The distance to the canyon floor lessens. But the way remains just as steep, too steep for you to risk climbing down. Nor do you find any more ladders.

The sun never sets on Utopa, so you have no way of judging time. You need to eat something. You've had nothing since your last vitro bar back on your ship. And you ate that at least ten hours before you landed. By now your body is beginning to feel numb, and your head aches.

The path along the rim of the cliff descends rapidly. You scramble down the trail, hardly caring where it leads . . . and reach the sea! All around you is sand, and beyond it, the freshwater ocean. You try to move toward the ocean, but your legs no longer obey your mind. You drop to your knees and begin to crawl. You never quite reach the water.

The End

For the next few months you live an easy, comfortable life in Ute's village. One day his scouts report that the eye ships have all gone away. With Ute and some others from the village, you set out to explore the surrounding countryside.

The land is as beautiful and unspoiled as ever. But you find neither Utopans nor any animals in your travels. Sadly, every person and creature outside the remote village seems to have starved.

You do find another A-3 Scout ship! It doesn't seem likely, but perhaps, like you, Mike Tanner survived somewhere in the wilderness. Though his Scout is too badly damaged to fly, the radio still works. You send out a distress signal. With luck your signal will be picked up, and a Federation ship will be sent to bring you home.

You look around at the grassy plains, the majestic river, and the lovely hills beyond. Utopa is once again a perfect planet—though a very lonely one, you think.

The End

You plunge into the water and make pretty good progress. But toward the middle of the river the current becomes much swifter. You're rapidly being swept downstream. In the distance, you hear rapids, and suddenly you remember having seen them from the rim of the canyon. You begin to panic!

If you turn so as to be swimming partly upstream but pointed toward your goal on the opposite shore, turn to page 70.

If you just keep pointed straight across the river as if there were no current at all, turn to page 114.

104

For the next three Earth days you spend a lot of time in front of the video screen watching the computer reconstruction of activity on Utopa. Kodor's huge command ship, fully visible, hovers above the planet's surface. You watch with fascination as robots with specialized attachments dig up slaif plants, bundle their root systems, and bring them inside the alien vessel. Within three days, seven hundred plants are taken, all removed from a single large grove, one of thousands scattered about on the planet. Meanwhile the eye ships return to the command ship, gliding effortlessly and silently into its cavernous bays. The command ship lifts off, becoming invisible almost as soon as it clears the treetops. Using infrared sensors, Federation Command is able to monitor the ship's path—toward the star Aldeberan—for only a few million miles.

Turn to page 23.

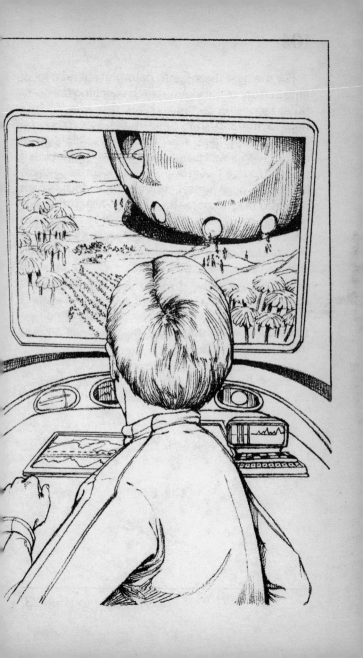

Nearly ten years pass before a passing Scout craft sends back new word about Utopa. You're now president of the entire Federation and, of course, extremely busy with your work. At first you toss the dispatch aside. You don't really want to read about the Utopans and other animals that must have starved as the three-horned zetkgees overran the island-continent. Then curiosity gets the better of you, and you pick up the dispatch:

TO FEDERATION COMMAND:
RE: UTOPA

Upon landing, I found that the Utopans and other animals were all alive and in good condition. The excess zetkgees died from eating a plant that was harmless to all other forms of life. This plant had sprung up where large areas had been stripped of slaif by the zetkgees. Slaif is now growing back everywhere, and Utopa is growing more perfect every day.

Scout A-7

The End

As you continue upstream above the rapids, the trail grows steeper and rougher. Eventually you reach a sheer rock wall. At one time it would have been impossible to climb. But it's now so pockmarked by erosion, you're able to find plenty of footholds and handholds.

In the light gravity of Utopa, the climb is easier than you'd thought it would be. You're so impressed by how fast you can climb that you forget to be careful. A few feet from the top you slip. In a moment you're tumbling back to the bottom. Fortunately your fall is broken by a thick bush. Bruised and shaken, you feel your aching leg and ankle and rub your elbow. You're thankful that gravity is much weaker on Utopa than on Earth. Otherwise, you never would have survived the fall.

You're trying to decide whether to attempt the climb again, when you spot another trail. You follow it as it twists and turns and finally heads downstream.

Turn to page 46.

But you can't let your guard down now. You'll have to think hard if you're going to outwit Kodor. "I don't think Earthlings will be as frightened by your eye ships as the Utopans were," you say.

Kodor looks at you intently. "That may be so. There is no one mythology we can use against Earth. Our monitors have gathered every scrap of information about your planet. Our computers know more about Earth than you Earthlings know."

"Then you should realize that Earthlings are heavily armed," you say.

"That will pose no problem for me," Kodor says. "Our technology is far superior."

"Then what do you want of us?"

"You will bring to your people videotapes showing our military superiority. Because you are a person whose loyalty to Earth could never be in doubt, they will believe you. Then, Earth and its Federation will surrender to us without my having to damage my future property."

"What if we refuse?" you ask boldly.

"If you refuse, you shall die, and I shall conquer Earth anyway. And there will be a great deal more suffering."

You think as hard as you can. You've got to come up with a way to stop Kodor from carrying out his evil plan.

Turn to page 60.

You pass your hand across your forehead, brushing away the sweat that has formed there. How tragic that such great power has fallen into the hands of an insane creature! *"Killing the creatures on this planet is not the most efficient thing to do,"* you radio back.

"Why not?" Kodor asks. *"It must be—I always do the most efficient thing."*

"It's not," you reply. *"There's so much slaif on this planet that the Utopans can easily spare seven hundred plants. In fact, if you ask them nicely, I'm sure they'll dig the plants and load them aboard your ship. And because they know these plants so well, they're less likely to injure them. That would be the most efficient way!"*

There's a long pause; then you hear Kodor's voice again. *"Though you are nothing more than a barbarian to us, Earthling, what you say is logical, and, since I am always logical, I shall do as you suggest."*

Shortly afterward, Zarg Tanz, Kodor's ambassador, lands nearby in a shuttle craft, and you introduce him to the Utopan leaders. Once reassured that they will not be harassed by the evil eye, the Utopans are more than willing to provide Kodor with the seven hundred slaif plants he wants.

Once the eye ship has been removed, the gentle Utopans go back to work and quickly restore the health of all creatures. Soon Utopa is once again the perfect planet.

Turn to page 82.

110

Speechless, you stare at the woman. You're appalled that the Utopans have been hiding from something called the evil eye—superstitiously believing that it will place a terrible curse on them.

"Listen to me, friends," you finally say. "Your fear is the worst curse of all. You and all the other creatures on the planet are starving because you're afraid to harvest slaif!"

The Utopans perk up a little as you speak. They can't ignore your earnestness, but still they shake their heads. Their senseless fear is too deeply rooted. You glance at their powerful, curved nails, genetically fashioned for one purpose: paring the slaif root, something no other creature on Utopa—including you—can do.

Desperately, you try to think. Time is short. Soon these Utopans will be too weak to pare slaif. Then all will be lost.

If you tell the Utopans that the evil eye has left and it's safe to come out, turn to page 30.

If you try to convince them that they must not be afraid of the evil eye, turn to page 53.

A few weeks later word spreads throughout Utopa that the eye ships have gone. They've departed as mysteriously as they'd arrived. Not everyone survived the catastrophe the ships provoked. But for those who did, life has been restored to its normal tranquillity and abundance. Utopa is once again the perfect planet.

The End

The river flows on toward the sea. Above you, the canyon walls are steep and forbidding. Occasionally your log passes a point of land close enough to swim to, but there would be little point in trying—you'd be hopelessly marooned. Better to stay on your "raft" and hope you'll find another settlement.

You doze off, and when you awaken you're no longer traveling through the canyon. Along the left bank of the river is a low forest of magony trees. On the right bank is a broad, grassy plain. The river is broader here, and the current is much slower. You guess that the sea lies not far ahead.

You're hungrier than ever, and although you feel somewhat rested from your long nap, you know your strength is waning. You strain your eyes, trying to see through the trees. You hope to glimpse a roof or a clearing, a sign of a Utopan village. Then, as you cast your eyes over the broad, grassy plain, your heart leaps. The cylindrical shape near the edge of the water is an A-3 Scout ship—it must be Mike Tanner's!

In a few minutes your log has drifted farther downstream until it's almost even with the Scout. This is no time for hesitation. You stand, balancing yourself on the floating log. Coiling your legs, you quickly dive. You hit the water flat, like a racer, with legs kicking. Stroking and breathing as efficiently as you can to conserve energy, you swim across the river. A few minutes later, exhausted but happy, you pull yourself up onto the grassy shore.

Turn to page 77.

114

By heading straight across the river instead of fighting the current, you conserve your strength and safely make it to the opposite shore. But you're much farther downstream—just a hundred yards or so above the rapids. Exhausted, you rest on the riverbank for a while. Then you start through the tall beach grass, searching for a good route to the Utopan village that you saw from the opposite side of the canyon.

You soon find an animal trail leading in the right direction and follow it eagerly. You haven't gone far when you're stopped by a sight that wrenches your heart. Several half-starved walities lie panting in the tall grass. These sweet-faced, aquatic creatures, not much more agile on land than sea lions, must have left the river to search for the Utopans who would normally come to the riverbank to feed them. You move past them, quickening your stride. You're more anxious than ever to find the Utopans and do what you can to reverse the tragedy that's turning the perfect planet into a planet of doom. But soon you realize that the trail has turned. It's looping back in a downsteam direction. You're exhausted, famished, and lost, moving now out of sheer desperation.

Turn to page 12.

What will happen when there's no longer enough slaif for the Utopans and other animals to eat? you wonder. Surely the outcome will be catastrophic. There's little doubt in your mind that the mumpa beasts will go crazy with frustration, just as they did when Kodor terrorized the planet many years ago.

You have a warm spot in your heart for Utopa. You saved it once before, and you're determined to do what you can to save it again. It takes only a few days to clear your desk and plan your mission. Soon you're on your way, traveling at metaspeed aboard the Federation's flagship, *Omricon*, heading for Utopa.

Turn to page 85.

A cheer goes up throughout the *Rama*, but it's cut off abruptly when a synthesized, projected voice fills the room.

"This is the voice of Aldeberan, lord of the galaxy. In destroying Kodor you destroyed nothing more than a fly. Having shown yourselves to be creatures that snap at flies, you have proved yourselves on a level with frogs. Return to Earth. Henceforth it shall be your pond. Never Venture Forth Again."

"What is this?" Admiral Gordon yells. "We're not going to follow these orders!"

But already some mysterious force has set the *Rama* in motion toward Earth. The crew struggles in vain to regain control of the ship. The admiral's eyes meet yours. You know you won't see the perfect planet again.

The End

ABOUT THE AUTHOR

EDWARD PACKARD is a graduate of Princeton University and Columbia Law School. He developed the unique storytelling approach used in the Choose Your Own Adventure series while thinking up stories for his children, Caroline, Andrea, and Wells.

ABOUT THE ILLUSTRATOR

LESLIE MORRILL is a designer and illustrator whose work has won him numerous awards. He has illustrated over thirty books for children, including the Bantam Classic edition of *The Wind in the Willows*. Mr. Morrill has illustrated *Indian Trail, Attack of the Monster Plants, The Owl Tree, Sand Castle, Light on Burro Mountain,* and *Home in Time for Christmas,* in the Skylark Choose Your Own Adventure series, and *Lost on the Amazon, Mountain Survival, Invaders of the Planet Earth, The Brilliant Dr. Wogan,* and *The First Olympics* in the Choose Your Own Adventure series.